Twins

MIKE CICCOTELLO

Farrar Straus Giroux
New York

Farrar Straus Giroux Books for Young Readers
An imprint of Macmillan Publishing Group, LLC
120 Broadway, New York, NY 10271

Color separations by Bright Arts (H.K.) Ltd.
Printed in China by Toppan Leefung Printing, Ltd.,
Dongguan City, Guangdong Province
Designed by Eileen Gilshian
First edition, 2019

1 3 5 7 9 10 8 6 4 2

mackids.com

Library of Congress Cataloging-in-Publication Data

Names: Ciccotello, Mike, author, illustrator. | Title: Twins / Mike Ciccotello.
Description: First edition. | New York : Farrar Straus Giroux, 2019. |
    Summary: A boy who plays everything from leap frog to piano duets with
    his twin brother loves being a twin, even when they disagree.
Identifiers: LCCN 2018060273 | ISBN 9780374312121 (hardcover)
Subjects: | CYAC: Twins—Fiction. | Brothers—Fiction.
Classification: LCC PZ7.1.C553 Twi 2019 | DDC [E]—dc23
LC record available at https://lccn.loc.gov/2018060273

Our books may be purchased in bulk for promotional, educational, or
business use. Please contact your local bookseller or the Macmillan Corporate
and Premium Sales Department at (800) 221-7945 ext. 5442 or by email at
MacmillanSpecialMarkets@macmillan.com.

For my sweet twins

—Dad

Being a twin is great.
Sometimes our friends can't tell us apart.

We always have a
pal for leapfrog,

piggyback rides,

and piano duets.

And we always have someone to talk to.

Twins enjoy a lot of the same things,
but we like to do them differently,

like riding trikes,

trick-or-treating,

and building snowmen.

Salad is our favorite food.
I like to take my time eating,
but my twin likes to finish first.

We both have serious dance moves.
I stay in one spot. My twin is all over
the place.

We also like to read, but in different ways.

Of course, twins don't always agree.
We argue over who draws better

and who is stronger.

Sometimes we even fight over
who gets to use the hammer.

When we have a disagreement,
it might last all afternoon

and turn into a big, rotten fight.

Sometimes twins just need to be apart for a little while.

But we can never stay mad for very long.

When we each want to do things our own way
and can't agree, it's good to compromise.

Sometimes we forget
that we work best together.

Being a twin has ups
and downs.

But in the end, we always see eye to eye.

It's great being a twin,
knowing there's someone who's just like you.